The Little Buddha
Finding Happiness

The Little Buddha
Finding Happiness

Claus Mikosch

Illustrations by Kate Chesterton

AMMONITE
PRESS

To friendship

This edition published 2019
by Ammonite Press
an imprint of Guild of Master Craftsman Publications Ltd
Castle Place, 166 High Street, Lewes,
East Sussex, BN7 1XU, United Kingdom
www.ammonitepress.com

First published by Verlag Herder

Text © Claus Mikosch, 2019
Illustrations © Kate Chesterton, 2019
Copyright in the Work © GMC Publications Ltd, 2019

ISBN 978 1 78145 379 7

A catalogue record for this book is available from the British Library.

Publisher: Jason Hook
Design Manager: Robin Shields
Editor: Jamie Pumfrey

Colour reproduction by GMC Reprographics
Printed and bound in China

FSC
www.fsc.org
MIX
Paper from
responsible sources
FSC® C016973

Contents

Chapter 1
The Little Buddha

nce upon a time, there was a Little Buddha who lived in a faraway land. His home was a flat stone under a big old Bodhi tree and, as you might imagine, the Little Buddha did what all Little Buddhas do: he meditated all day long.

While in meditation he breathed deeply, in and out, without thinking about anything in particular. His heart beat peacefully and his whole body was still. Sometimes he would watch the clouds during his meditations, the way they would slowly roll by, but most of the time he had his eyes closed and only listened to the sounds of the invisible wind. He even spent the nights like this.

The Little Buddha enjoyed meditating and he also loved the peaceful spot under the big old Bodhi tree. Yet, at the same time, he also felt that something was missing in his life. Something very important; something that neither the clouds in the sky nor the trees on the ground were able to give him. Something that couldn't be replaced by anything, something that everybody needed in order to live happily. For quite a while he had been trying desperately to live without this something, but all his attempts had failed miserably. Even his calm breathing, which was usually the answer to every problem, could not help him. What the Little Buddha was missing was contact with other people. Most of the time he was completely alone.

He only had one friend, a farmer who lived about an hour's walk away. But the farmer was a very busy man; from dawn to dusk he had to work on his fields. And apart from the farmer, there was no-one else who came to visit him under his tree.

Of course, there were also many moments when the Little Buddha enjoyed being alone. But all the time? Every day, every night, always alone? No, even for him that was too much solitude. After all, the Little Buddha was a human being like everybody else, and there is nobody in the whole wide world who enjoys being alone all the time.

*

One day, when the farmer was paying him one of his rare and brief visits, the Little Buddha lost his patience.

'I am absolutely fed up with being alone!' he said with great frustration.

'How come?' the farmer asked in surprise. 'I thought that you enjoyed the solitude.'

'Yes, sometimes that's true. But not always.' The Little Buddha seemed desperate and sad.

His friend, the farmer, wanted to help him but he didn't know how. He himself had to work almost all the time so couldn't visit him more often. But suddenly he had an idea.

'Why don't you go on holiday?'

The Little Buddha was puzzled.

'You want me to go on holiday?'

'Yes, why not? Go and travel for a while. Look at what else is happening in the world. You know, when you travel you always get to meet lots of different people, and from other people you can learn a lot about life. And you will also have a lot of company. You won't be alone so much, and this is exactly what you want, isn't it?'

The deep desperation the Little Buddha had been feeling only moments before was slowly being replaced by some confidence.

'Going on a journey...' he thought to himself.

'Getting to know other people...'

A smile returned to his face.

'You know, this is an excellent idea. I will leave first thing tomorrow morning.'

The farmer was happy because the Little Buddha was feeling better. After all, there is hardly anything worse than not being able to help a friend who is really sad.

'Just make sure that you find the way back to your Bodhi tree one day,' said the farmer.

'Of course I will come back,' the Little Buddha said. 'But first I will get to know the world. I'm already excited about who I'm going to meet on my journey. Thank you so much for your help, my friend. You are right, sometimes a Little Buddha should go on holiday too.'

*

As he led such a simple life, the Little Buddha didn't have to make many travel preparations. The farmer had given him a useful shoulder bag as a gift, and into this bag he put a blanket for cold nights, a few apples for the first part of the journey and a small white stone to remind him of his home.

The following morning he said goodbye to the big old Bodhi tree, then set off. He started walking straight ahead in the direction in which the sun had just risen.

Admittedly he was a little nervous because he didn't know what was awaiting him, far away from home. But more than anything else he was happy that the farmer had thought of the holiday idea. Even though he was convinced that his home under the big old Bodhi tree was the most beautiful and most peaceful spot in the world, he also felt that a Buddha wasn't made to spend his whole life sitting under a tree.

His journey had begun.

Chapter 2
The Courageous Widow

fter travelling for half a day, the Little Buddha decided to have his first break. His feet were aching terribly because he wasn't used to walking such long distances – for the last few years he had been sitting under his Bodhi tree without really moving much at all.

Just after a crossroads, he left the path and walked a few steps down a slope to a small stream. It carried beautifully pure water from the nearby mountains. A cold refreshing drink was exactly what he needed. He quenched his thirst, then sat down on the soft grass next to the stream. He meditated for a while, enjoying the beautiful scenery and regaining some strength.

*

Once he had recovered, the Little Buddha climbed up the slope again. He was just about to continue his journey when he noticed a young woman coming towards him from the crossroads. Being curious by nature, he waited for her to reach him.

The woman was carrying a large bag in one hand, and with the other hand she was supporting a round basket, which she was balancing on her head.

'Hello,' the Little Buddha said.

'Hello,' the young woman replied as she was passing him.

The Little Buddha started to walk beside her.

'Wow, you have a lot of luggage. Do you want me to help you carry it?'

Now the woman stopped. She smiled and took the big round basket from her head.

'That would be very kind of you.'

She held one handle of the basket with her left hand, the Little Buddha held the other handle with his right hand, and like this they continued together on their way.

'Where are you going?' the Little Buddha wanted to know.

'To the big town,' the young woman said. 'And you?'

'I just walk straight ahead,' he answered cheerfully, 'wherever destiny takes me.'

'You don't know where you are going?'

'No. You see, I'm on holiday, and so it's not really important for me to know where I am going. The main thing is that I do something different from sitting alone all day long under my tree.'

The afternoon had just begun and a long journey was ahead of them. The Little Buddha didn't know anything about the big town, but he decided nevertheless to go along. Why not? After all he hadn't made any plans for his journey. He was happy to finally have some company. Besides, he could help the woman carry her baggage. It was a nice feeling to help somebody, to share the load.

'Where is your home?' he asked her.

'I come from a small village by the sea. I have lived there all my life, up until now.'

For a moment, the young woman was lost in thought. She seemed sad.

'Don't you like the sea any more?' the Little Buddha asked carefully.

'Oh no, I still love the sea. It's absolutely beautiful! But for the last few months I haven't felt content in my village. It didn't feel like home any longer, and because of that I am going to the big town now. It's time for a change.'

'Why didn't you feel content in your village any more?' the Little

Buddha asked, curious as he was.

'That's a long story. But as we have plenty of time, I'll tell it to you.'
So while they continued walking towards the big town, the young woman told her story to the Little Buddha.

*

When I was twenty years old I married my husband. We had a wonderful wedding in our village, a big celebration with all our friends and family. We were both very happy and wanted to have children. However, two years ago, my husband died suddenly. It was an accident, he sailed into a bad storm with his fishing boat and drowned. After a marriage of only one year, I became a widow overnight. My whole life was shattered that day, and for many weeks the only thing I could do was cry my eyes out.

After a few months of mourning I slowly recovered. I began to feel better again and I wanted to make a new start. After all, I was still alive. Yet very soon I realized that it was impossible to make a new start in my village. The people believed that a widow was supposed to spend the rest of her life in sorrow. This is what tradition said. I wasn't allowed to have another husband, I wasn't supposed to laugh or to be happy. I felt as if I had drowned too.

For some time, I complied with this tradition because I was too weak to object to everyone's opinion. But soon I realized that I had to make a decision: either to stay in my native village, alone and forever sad, or to start a new life in a different place, with the possibility of becoming happy again.

You know, I love my village, the sea and of course my friends and my family, but all this seems totally worthless to me if I am forced to live in sorrow. I often think about my late husband; I loved him very much, but I think I have mourned long enough. I want to look ahead now, and because I can't do this in my village, I have decided on a new beginning somewhere else. I have decided to open a completely new chapter in my book of life.

*

The Little Buddha had listened carefully. It was a sad story, but he admired the courage of the young woman. What he didn't understand, though, was the behaviour of the people who were closest to her.

'Why didn't your friends and your family help you? Do they want you to be sad for the rest of your life?'

The young woman hesitated for a moment before she answered.

'No, I don't think that they want me to be sad, but you are right, they didn't support me either. I think both my family and friends are too caught up with tradition. They are scared of making a mistake, scared of being suddenly alone with their opinion, without having the security of the whole village on their side. Because of this fear, they prefer to do everything the way they have always done it.'

The woman was silent for a moment.

'It's possible that all of the people in my village are happy living their lives like this. I don't know. But I do know that it's not the life that I want for myself.'

The Little Buddha knew that he wouldn't have been happy either if he had been in her situation. Thinking about it, he just hoped that he, too, would have had the courage needed to move on and make a new beginning, despite all of the difficulties.

'You know,' the young woman continued, 'there are certain things in life that you can't change, no matter how much you wish you could. You simply have to accept them the way they are. Other things you can change, and this is where you should concentrate your energy.

'My husband is dead. I can't change that, whether I like it or not. But I am alive, and it's up to me whether I lead a sad or a happy life.'

They stopped for a moment, looked at each other, and saw a happy smile on each other's faces. The young woman was glad that she had left her village, and therefore didn't have to be sad any more. The Little Buddha was glad that he had decided to go travelling, and therefore didn't have to be alone all the time.

They continued their journey in silence, both with the same thought:

'Sometimes you have to find the courage to take the first step.'

To choose a direction. To make a decision. And then to stop thinking and simply start.

Chapter 3
The Smart Professor

n the early evening the Little Buddha and the young woman arrived in a remote village. They had enough time to reach the big town, but they decided to stop and continue their journey the next day. Both of them were tired after walking all day.

Luckily there were still two beds available at the only guesthouse in the village. The friendly landlord gave them a warm welcome and showed them to their rooms. Afterwards, he started to prepare dinner for the hungry travellers. Soon the whole house was filled with the delicious smell of fresh, tasty food. And there was another highlight offered by the guesthouse: a terrace with a fantastic view over a beautiful valley.

So while the Little Buddha and the young woman were waiting for the food to be served, they made themselves comfortable in two hammocks on the terrace, enjoying the peaceful arrival of twilight. What a wonderful moment it was! After a long and hard day, there was nothing better than to relax with the slowly setting sun.

The food tasted even better than it smelt. The Little Buddha and the young woman felt as if they were in paradise. After they had finished their delicious dinner, they stayed a little longer at the table and drank some tea.

The Little Buddha was thinking about the town and wondering what it would be like. He had never been to a big town. He imagined it to be like ten huge villages put together. A massive, gigantic place, full of people and possibilities.

The young woman was looking forward to the big town, too, but at the same time she was also rather worried. She felt quite insecure because she didn't have a profession – she hadn't even attended school properly. Since childhood, she had helped with the general household tasks of washing, cleaning, cooking and so on, first in her parents' home and later in her husband's family home. She had never earned her own money, because she had never needed any, but now her situation was very different. She knew that she would need a lot of money to survive in the big town, and to earn money she needed a job.

'I don't know how I am supposed to find any work in the town,' she told the Little Buddha, who was still daydreaming about the possibilities of the gigantic village. 'You know, sometimes I feel quite hopeless when I think about the fact that I don't have any skills to help me get a paid job, as if I went fishing without a net or rod. How am I supposed to survive like this?'

The Little Buddha, having returned from his daydream, started pondering his new friend's worries. He was sure that there was an answer to her problem; that there was a way to help her feel less insecure.

While he was thinking about a possible solution, an old man suddenly came to their table. He was wearing round glasses and had a pipe sticking out of his mouth.

'Excuse me,' the man said with a strangely hesitant, yet also determined, voice. 'I was sitting at the table next to you and couldn't help listening to some of your conversation. If you allow me, I would like to tell you a story: a true story that a friend of mine told me not too long ago.'

The man took a puff on his pipe and gave them a questioning look. Trying to convince them, he added, 'It's a story about knowledge and skill.'

The young widow was slightly puzzled, and even a bit nervous. But she was also curious to find out why the man had approached them, and what it was that he had to say.

'May I?' the man asked, pointing to the free chair at their table.

Both the Little Buddha and the young woman nodded.

'Thank you,' the man said, and then he took a seat. 'I am sure that you'll like the story.'

Although they had never met him before they felt that the old man was trustworthy. There was something very calm, and also something very fascinating, about him.

'I am intrigued,' the young woman said with a careful smile.

The old man took another long puff on his pipe and then he began the story.

*

Many years ago a sailing boat called Desperado was crossing the ocean from one side to the other. On board were the captain and his crew, the freight and one travelling professor. The professor had been researching for two years and was returning home.

On the long voyage across the ocean, the captain and his crew often gathered in the professor's cabin to learn from his wisdom.

Sometimes the professor tested their general knowledge.

'Tell me, what do you know about geography?' he asked them.

'We don't know what that is,' they answered.

'What? You don't know what geography is? Well, geography is the science of the Earth. I wonder what you have done with your lives...'

The captain and his crew felt ashamed. What had they done with their lives? Why didn't they know what geography was? They all felt very stupid.

A few days later they gathered again in the professor's cabin, and again the professor tested their knowledge about the world.

'Now tell me, what do you know about mathematics?'

'We have no idea what that is.'

'What? You also don't know what mathematics is? You must be joking! Mathematics is the science of numbers. You have wasted all your life not knowing this, I can't believe it.'

The captain and his crew were now even more ashamed. It seemed as if they were indeed stupid, and suddenly their lives seemed completely worthless.

A few days later everybody was sitting in the professor's cabin once again.

'Let me ask you another question: what do you know about biology?'

'Please tell us, we don't have a clue.'

'You don't know what biology is either? Biology is the science of cells and of animals and... What do you actually know? As I have told you before, you have wasted your whole lives.'

The captain and his crew were once again very ashamed, and by now they even felt a little depressed. What had they done with their lives?

Two days later, the Desperado was sailing through a big storm. Suddenly one of the sailors came running to the professor's cabin and knocked loudly on the door.

'Professor, come out quickly!'

The professor opened his door.

'How dare you interrupt my studies! What do you want?'

'The storm has damaged the boat very badly. We all have to jump overboard and swim for our lives.'

'Hmmm... Swimming? I don't know how to swim.'

'No? Professor, in that case you have a big problem... You've wasted your whole life!'

*

All three were silent for a while.

'That's a really good story,' the Little Buddha said eventually.

'Yes, it's a great story,' the young woman continued, 'but unfortunately it also confirms my insecurity. The way I understand it, you shouldn't cross the ocean on a boat if you can't swim. So if you don't know anything about science, maybe you shouldn't go and live in a big town.'

The young widow looked questioningly at the old storyteller.

'Or am I wrong?'

'I understand what you're saying, and no, you are not totally wrong. Every person usually learns exactly what he or she needs for a particular life situation: special knowledge that is needed for survival. In order to survive in a big town, the knowledge that you need is very different from that which you need when leading a life on the ocean. At the end of the day this is the moral of the story: knowledge is absolutely relative! It always depends on the situation.'

The old man lit his pipe again.

'But don't worry, you can still go into town without having to be scared. There is just one rule: be prepared to learn new things!'

For a moment there was silence again at the table. Then the old man continued speaking.

'The professor was very arrogant and always acted as if he knew everything that could be known in the world. He didn't show any interest in the lives of the captain or the sailors, nor in their stories or their knowledge of life on the ocean. It was quite the contrary; he treated them in a humiliating, disrespectful way. If he had listened for once, instead of constantly speaking and teaching, then maybe he would have learned that the most important thing in the life of a seaman is to know how to swim. And if he had shown some interest then maybe one of the sailors would have taught him the science of swimming. But the professor hadn't been prepared to learn, he only wanted to teach.'

The Little Buddha and the young woman understood the words of the stranger. Of course, the big town was going to be a great challenge for them, but there was indeed no reason to be afraid, especially not on account of a lack of knowledge, because knowledge could be gained.

'It's actually quite simple,' the old man said, while getting up from his chair and taking another puff on his pipe.

'All you have to do is to approach the new situation with an open mind. Be curious and show respect to all of the people that you meet. And trust, because everything will unfold as it should.'

Then he disappeared just as suddenly as he had arrived.

*

The following morning the young woman and the Little Buddha continued their journey after a restful night. The path they were walking on gradually changed into a big road and they met many other people who were also travelling into the big town.

While getting closer and closer to their destination with every step, the Little Buddha was thinking about the previous evening. He wondered whether the young woman was still worried about her situation.

'How do you feel about the big town now? Did the old man's story help you at all?'

'Oh yes, it helped a lot.' The young woman already seemed much more positive. 'I still don't know how I can earn the money I need, but the man has given me some courage and some confidence that I will find a way. So instead of worries, I now carry hope with me.'

The Little Buddha smiled.

'I am convinced that you have a good chance of finding work. If you really expect something good to happen, then you will encounter exactly that.'

*

At midday they arrived in the town. Although they had become good friends within a short period of time, the Little Buddha and the young woman decided to go their separate ways again. They wanted to explore the town by themselves.

'I hope that you will have many great experiences on your trip,' the young woman said.

'And I hope that you will be happier in the town than you have been in your village. I thank you for your company, and for sharing part of your journey with me.'

A tear was running down the young woman's cheek as they hugged each other to say goodbye.

'Take care,' she said. 'Until we meet again one day.'

'Yes, until we meet again,' the Little Buddha replied. 'And always remember: roam the world with open ears so that you will hear what life wants to tell you.'

Chapter 4
The Unsuccessful Merchant

verything was even bigger, louder and faster than the Little Buddha had imagined. The town was bubbling like a volcano that was about to erupt. In every corner there were people, horse-drawn carriages were criss-crossing every street, cows were roaming about. It was total chaos taking place right in front of his very eyes. Yet amidst all this hectic confusion, there was a seemingly endless number of fascinating things to be discovered and absorbed, especially for someone who had spent most of his life meditating under a lonely tree.

For example, the Little Buddha had never seen a shop where you could buy flowers. He didn't really understand why you should pay money for flowers; after all, they were growing for free in every field. How strange, he thought to himself, but still it was fascinating.

Something he admired – or, even better, something he adored – were the countless clothing shops on almost every corner. You could buy clothes in every imaginable colour and shape. For him, the choice was absolutely mind-blowing.

Another thing he soon noticed in the town was that everybody was constantly on the move. Nobody was ever still, not even for a moment. Either the people were running around like crazy ants, or they were talking to somebody, or they were eating, or they were drinking, or they were busy in some other way. Even those people who weren't doing anything in particular appeared to be always occupied with something, as if they were searching inside their heads for some hidden thoughts.

'No matter what the townspeople are doing, they are never really quiet,' he realized in disbelief.

After some time, the Little Buddha arrived at a crowded market where local merchants were selling fresh fruit and vegetables. While he was walking around, always observant of the many things happening around him, he noticed that almost all the merchants had exactly the same products. He wanted to buy an apple, but he had no idea how to choose between the many stalls. So instead of trying to make a conscious decision, he simply went to the first stall that he saw. He stopped in front of a huge mountain of fruit.

His big eyes stared at the incredibly large selection.

'I would like a nice apple,' the Little Buddha said.

'Would you prefer a sweet or a sour one?' the merchant asked.

'I think I want a sweet one, but the best thing would be to have an apple that is both sweet and sour at the same time.'

'No problem,' said the merchant, and passed him a beautiful red apple. 'You're new in town, aren't you?'

'How could you tell?' the Little Buddha wondered in naive surprise.

'Well, you hardly ever see anybody strolling around the market in such a relaxed way. Here in the town, nobody has that much time.'

'You are right, I have noticed this too. What a pity.'

The Little Buddha took a big bite from his apple, chewing it with great pleasure.

'I think this is one of the best apples I've ever tasted.'

The merchant smiled modestly.

For a while they both stood there in silence and watched the hustle and bustle of the market. Suddenly the Little Buddha realized that he didn't have anywhere to sleep that night.

'Do you know where I can find a place to stay for tonight?'

'If you want you can stay at my house,' the merchant replied. 'I have enough space. It wouldn't be any problem.'

'Thank you, that would be great.'

The Little Buddha then remembered the words of the old man in the guesthouse: 'Be open, be curious and trust, because everything will unfold as it should.'

The man had been right; the town had welcomed him with open arms.

*

At first he had intended to stay only one night in the town, but soon the Little Buddha realized that he needed more time. There was so much to do and so much to see, and so many interesting people to encounter. The town offered him an excitement that he had never experienced before, and he wanted more of it. And so, as the merchant was happy to share his home a bit longer, the Little Buddha decided to stay.

Sometimes, of course, he thought of his own home under the big old Bodhi tree, but it was still much too early to return. After all, his journey had only just begun.

*

One evening, coming back from one of his explorations of the town, the Little Buddha saw the merchant sitting in a corner of his house with a gloomy look on his face.

'What's wrong?' the Little Buddha asked.

The friendly merchant hesitated for a moment before looking up.

'You know, I don't have any success with my market stall. I am really worried. The people seem to be going to all the other stalls apart from mine.'

'That's not true. After all, I came to your stall.'

'Yes, but that was just luck, and recently good luck hasn't visited me very often.'

The merchant sounded desperate, and indeed in comparison to other market stalls he had very few customers. For some reason, the people stayed away.

'Do you believe in luck?' the Little Buddha asked all of a sudden.

The merchant stared back at him. He didn't know what to say.

After a few moments of silence, the Little Buddha picked up the conversation again.

'You know, I don't believe in luck,' he said. 'Neither in good luck nor in bad luck. I think you always find what you are looking for.'

Now the merchant stared even more.

'I get the feeling that you don't really want to work on the market.'

The merchant didn't say a word, but his silence confirmed the feeling of his guest. Over the preceding days, the Little Buddha had already noticed that there was something wrong with the merchant. He was always extremely friendly, but he didn't seem happy.

'I think that you are looking for something that you won't find with your market stall, and that's probably also the reason why you don't have much success. If you do something that you don't really want to be doing, it is very difficult to be successful at it.'

'Yes, but it's not as easy as you might imagine.' The merchant had stopped staring. 'I have to earn money, and that's why I am on the market, selling fruit and vegetables. What I really want is not that important. After all, I have to live from something.'

'I understand that. But forget about the money for just one moment...'

'How can I forget about money when I need it to live?'

'Try, just for a moment,' the Little Buddha persisted. 'I am sure that you have some unfulfilled dreams.'

'I don't know.' It had been a long time since the merchant had thought about what he liked doing, and what made him happy. All his thoughts had centred around the market stall. There had been neither time nor space for dreams.

'I love to write,' he said eventually. 'And I love music. When I was younger, I used to say to myself that I would write a book about music one day.'

'And do you still want to do that?'

'Yes, eventually.'

'Why don't you do it now?'

'Because…'

The merchant was about to reply, but he couldn't find any words.

'If you wrote a book about music,' the Little Buddha continued, 'if you did something that you enjoyed doing, you would live a much happier life, and as a consequence more people on the market would come to you to buy their fruit and vegetables.'

'But I still wouldn't want to be on the market, so why should anything change?'

'Because people feel attracted by somebody who is happy. I think it is human nature. You always try to go where there is a chance of encountering happiness.'

The merchant had to agree with the Little Buddha. After all, who wanted to be in bad company? Nobody, especially not while shopping at the market.

Though one thing remained that the merchant didn't understand.

'And what about you? I wasn't happy, yet still you came to my stall.'

'Yes, that's true,' said the Little Buddha. 'But I think we have attracted each other for different reasons. Why don't you see it like this: I was looking for a place to sleep, and you were looking for somebody who would remind you of your dreams so that you can lead a happier life. In the end we have both found what we were looking for.'

They smiled for a moment, but quickly the doubts returned to the merchant's head.

'But when am I supposed to write the book? I have no time. As I said before, I have to earn money.'

'Yes, but I didn't say that you have to give up your work on the market. What about the time after work?'

The Little Buddha paused for a moment to carefully phrase what he wanted to say.

'When you come home from work you always seem very busy, but if you are honest with yourself you have to admit that you are not really doing anything. At least nothing that is important. I understand that you need to relax after a hard day's work, but why don't you use at least some of that time to write? It requires some initial effort, true, just like it used to for me when I first started meditating. But eventually, once you get into a rhythm, it will become a natural part of your life. In this way you will have something to look forward to during those long days on the market.'

The Little Buddha could see how the merchant was trying to find an excuse, but he wasn't successful.

'You are right,' he finally admitted.

*

And so, the same evening, the merchant started to write a book: a story about a small group of street musicians who travelled from town to town.

The merchant was enjoying his new task. During the day he worked on the market as usual, selling fruit and vegetables. Whenever it was quiet and he had nothing to do, he thought about the storyline of his book. Once a day he took a break for half an hour, just as he had always done. However, instead of sitting down and reading the newspaper as before, now he went to the far western side of the market where street musicians played for the passers-by. For the merchant, it was the perfect inspiration for his book. In the evenings, he sat down in front of a stack of paper and started writing.

Although he had changed neither the prices nor anything else, the merchant soon noticed that more people were coming to his stall. The words of his new friend were confirmed: intuitively most people did indeed prefer to go to places where they would encounter a happy person.

*

A few days later the merchant arrived at his home and told the Little Buddha that a woman had come to his stall that day asking him why he was so happy.

'And what did you tell her?'

'That I am happy because every day I do a little bit of something that I enjoy.'

The merchant was so enthusiastic about his new task that he didn't have any more reasons to be sad or in a bad mood.

'Today, I even thought that I could sell my book once it's ready. If it goes well, I won't have to work on the market any more, then I can write much more.'

He was already envisioning a successful future as a professional writer.

'Yes, maybe you could really sell your book,' the Little Buddha said. 'And I am sure that you can write much more. But I would be careful about giving up the market stall.'

'But why?' the merchant wondered in disbelief.

The Little Buddha looked deep into his friend's eyes.

'Well, who knows what other people you might still meet there...'

Chapter 5
The Man
Without Time

he Little Buddha was fascinated by the town. Not that he would have wanted to live there, but it was incredible how much there was to see and to explore. And he was especially taken by the people. There were so many different people. Big ones, small ones, fat ones, thin ones, pretty ones, ugly ones, rich ones, poor ones, friendly ones, nasty ones, happy ones, sad ones, clever ones, crazy ones and many, many more. Strangely enough, there were even lonely people amidst the masses.

*

One of these lonely people was a man called Mr Singer. Mr Singer was not only lonely, he was also extremely hectic. Or, more precisely, he was lonely because he was extremely hectic.

Mr Singer was unable to remain quietly in the same position for even a minute. When he was sitting, he was constantly see-sawing on his chair. When he was standing, he was swaying backwards and forwards all the time; and when he wasn't moving in one way or the other, he was talking, continuously, without drawing breath, and very fast.

The Little Buddha met Mr Singer for the first time in a chai-house. While he was living with the merchant, he had become accustomed to drinking chai, a refreshing tea, for breakfast. After he had tried a few different chai-houses he finally decided on the one that he liked the most, and he returned to it every day. He was sitting in this chai-house one morning when Mr Singer rushed in and ordered some tea.

Mr Singer took his chai and went to sit on one of the many stools. He placed his cup on a small side table and began to read his book. He was reading so quickly that it seemed as if he had to finish the whole book within an hour. While reading he was, of course, also see-sawing constantly on his chair.

The Little Buddha watched the hectic man for quite a while. As he was always interested in talking to other people, he eventually asked him why he was reading so quickly.

Mr Singer looked up without interrupting his see-saw motion, and noticed the Little Buddha sitting on the stool next to him.

'Because I don't have any time,' he answered very briefly.

'And why don't you have any time?' the Little Buddha wanted to know, but he didn't get any answer. Mr Singer got up all of a sudden, paid for his chai, quickly said goodbye to the chai-house owner, said 'I have to go' to the Little Buddha, then disappeared into the morning crowd on the street.

'What a strange man,' the Little Buddha thought.

*

Two days later exactly the same situation occurred. The Little Buddha was sitting in front of his chai when Mr Singer rushed in, quickly drank his tea, said he didn't have any time and stormed out of the cosy chai-house again.

'This guy is really weird,' the Little Buddha said to himself.

The next day the same scenario was unfolding. Mr Singer came in, ordered his chai and took a seat on one of the stools, wobbling away. He took out his book and started to speed-read just as before. After a few minutes, the Little Buddha made another attempt to talk to him. But the result was initially the same as before.

'I don't have time.'

'Never?'

'No, never.'

'But why not?' the Little Buddha persisted.

'Okay then,' Mr Singer finally said. 'I will quickly explain it to you.'

'Thank you.' The Little Buddha felt relieved. It had taken him three attempts to get that far.

'I'm a traveller,' Mr Singer said.

'Me too!' the Little Buddha exclaimed joyfully. He had already met three other travellers in the town, and talking to them had always been something special. He had learned about other exciting towns, about the sea and the mountains. He had heard fascinating, funny and also strange stories, and he had been told the best spots to enjoy the most beautiful sunsets. The Little Buddha therefore had many reasons to be excited.

Mr Singer, however, wasn't excited at all.

'How come you are asking me? If you are a traveller you should know yourself.' He didn't understand.

'What am I supposed to know?' the Little Buddha asked, cluelessly.

'That every journey means a lot of work. And all the work takes up a lot of time. After all, everything has to be organized and prepared very thoroughly.'

The Little Buddha continued with his questioning look, still not having any idea what the busy man was talking about.

Mr Singer shook his head. For him, it was completely and utterly incomprehensible that the Little Buddha couldn't relate to what he was saying.

'First of all, the exact route has to be planned, this is the most time-consuming part. I, for example, read all the books about my destination

that I can find in the library. Afterwards, accommodation has to be arranged, and then all possible information about all the different sights has to be gathered.'

He knocked back his chai as impatiently as ever, ordered another one and then continued to shake his head in disbelief.

'I really don't understand. You should know how long all of this takes. Just thinking about packing the bags is enough.'

He paused.

'Are you sure that you are a traveller?'

The Little Buddha seemed doubtful for a moment.

'I think so,' he said hesitantly.

'You think so? Does this mean yes or no?'

'Well, if a traveller is somebody who travels, then I am a traveller, yes.'

Now it was Mr Singer who felt a little insecure. He had to think.

'And are you sure that you don't have a time problem?'

'Why should I have a time problem?' the Little Buddha asked in astonishment. 'There is enough time. It just depends what you do with it.'

'Yes, but like it or not, certain things have to be done. Because I have to do so much, it seems to me as if there aren't enough hours in the day.'

Suddenly he stopped see-sawing on his stool.

'If only it were possible to buy hours somewhere!'

The Little Buddha stared at him in disbelief.

'Do you think this would solve your time problem?'

'I don't know. It depends how many hours I could buy.'

They both laughed. Fortunately, there was enough time for this despite all the rush.

'Why do you make so many plans anyway?' the Little Buddha asked after a brief pause.

'Because I am a traveller.'

Mr Singer continued to wobble nervously.

'And as I have told you already, there are certain preparations and plans that have to be made. It's what you are supposed to do.'

'Says who?'

'I don't know. But that's how it is.'

The Little Buddha started to get seriously concerned about Mr Singer.

'But why? This doesn't make any sense. Look at me: I am a traveller and I have hardly made any preparations at all.'

'Well, you are an exception then,' was the only answer that Mr Singer could come up with. And then, before the Little Buddha had a chance to deepen the discussion any further, the conversation was suddenly over.

'I really have to go now,' the bustling man said abruptly, cutting his neighbour short.

He quickly finished his second chai, got up and said goodbye.

The Little Buddha thanked Mr Singer for taking the time to talk to him and told him that he hoped to meet up again soon.

'Maybe you can tell me something about your travels the next time. About all the places that you have been to, and all the experiences that you have had.'

Mr Singer, who was already leaving the chai-house like a crazy whirlwind, stopped and turned around.

'All the places that I have been to?'

He was stunned and stared motionless at the Little Buddha.

'What do you mean? I haven't been anywhere yet. No time!'

*

After this bizarre experience with Mr Singer, the Little Buddha decided to leave the town and continue on his travels. He had enjoyed the excitement and the chaos, but he felt that life in the town was too fast for him. Somebody who was used to spending most of his time in solitude under a tree, in the most peaceful of surroundings, eventually starts to crave some slowness. There were many nice people in the town, but unfortunately many of them somehow seemed to confuse life with a race. 'Everywhere there's so much hustle and bustle,' the Little Buddha thought to himself. 'I wonder why people can't stop and stand still for once. Why does life have to be such a rush?'

It was as if God was waiting at the end of life with a running hourglass in his hand.

*

The next morning, the Little Budda said goodbye to the merchant. They were both sad that their paths were going separate ways again, but at the same time they were happy to have met at all. The two friends hugged and wished each other all the best.

The Little Buddha didn't have any special destination in mind for the next stage of his trip, all he knew was that he wanted to go to a place where it was quieter, and he also wanted to meet more people. For him it didn't really matter about getting to a particular place, he just wanted to experience travelling itself. So he just set off.

Past the shops and chai-houses, past all of the different squares and temples. Away from the hectic town, always straight on.

Headfirst into a new chapter of his journey.

The Man Without Time

Chapter 6
The Blind Witch

fter walking for quite some time past wide and open fields, the Little Buddha arrived at a big forest. Thousands of massive trees stood close to each other, swallowing almost all of the daylight. Everything was veiled in darkness. He stopped and looked around him. The path led right into the forest, straight into nothingness. It was spooky and mysterious, but nevertheless he decided to continue.

Just before he reached the outskirts of the woods, he saw a young woman entering the deep darkness without any sign of hesitation.

'It must be safe,' he thought to himself. Besides, he had become curious again, and so there wasn't really any possibility of turning around. He too entered the blackness of the forest and followed the path.

*

Soon, however, the Little Buddha had to stop again because he wasn't able to see a thing. His eyes needed some time to adjust to the dark, but once he could orientate himself he continued slowly along the path.

After he had covered some distance, he suddenly saw a column of light shining in the midst of the darkness. He was mesmerized by the bright light and continued walking towards it. When he got closer, he realized that it was a clearing. In an area the size of a small house, there were no trees, and so the sunlight reached the floor of the forest. The clearing was a few metres away from the path. While the Little Buddha was contemplating whether to stop and explore the clearing, he heard voices coming from that direction. He walked closer and was able to make out four people – three women and one man. One of them he recognized immediately. It was the woman he had seen not long before on the outskirts of the woods. She was sitting with the others on the exposed root of a very old tree, and they all seemed to be waiting for something.

When they noticed the Little Buddha, they greeted him in a friendly way and offered him a place next to them.

'Take a seat here. It will still take quite a while for you,' one of the women said.

The Little Buddha looked around, wondering.

'What is going to take a while for me?'

'Well, to speak to the witch. Or isn't that the reason you've come here?'

Now the three women and the man returned his questioning look.

'A witch? No, that's not why I came here.' He paused. 'Where is she supposed to be?'

One of the women turned around and without saying a word she pointed into the middle of the dark woods. The Little Buddha followed the direction she was pointing towards with his eyes, but apart from trees he couldn't see anything. He moved closer, but still he saw neither a witch nor anything else worth his attention.

'But where?' he asked again.

'On the ground,' the man said. 'You have to look very closely.'

The Little Buddha walked even further into the woods and then, all of a sudden, he discovered a hole in the ground. He tiptoed towards it and saw steps leading deep down into the earth. Next to the first step there was a big stone with something written on it. He leaned forward and read:

'In life you only ever see what you want to see.'

The Little Buddha's curiosity increased tremendously. Who was this witch? He turned around, absorbed in deep thought, and went back to the others who were still sitting on the root of the old tree.

'Does the witch live down there?'

'Yes,' one of the women answered, 'she has lived down there in her cave for over twenty years.'

'And why does she live in a cave? Isn't the forest dark enough already?'

'She doesn't mind,' the woman replied. 'She's blind.'

For a moment they all remained silent. Only the sounds of the woods were to be heard: the rustling of leaves and the sporadic creaking of old branches; the slight but constant buzzing of the insects; the gentle singing of the birds. It was quiet, but not completely still.

The man rose to speak.

'You are probably wondering why we are all waiting for the witch, aren't you?'

The Little Buddha nodded.

'The blind witch is a very wise woman who helps the people when they face a crisis in their lives. Even in the big town she is very well-known. Every day many people, just like us, come with different problems and receive her help.

'Why don't you visit her as well? She's a very interesting person, you won't be disappointed.'

The Little Buddha didn't have to think twice. Of course he waited.

*

The last rays of sunlight were illuminating the clearing when it was finally the Little Buddha's turn. The man was the last to leave the cave and told him that the witch was waiting for him. So the Little Buddha entered the dark hole and went underground.

*

'Welcome,' he heard a voice say even before he had reached the bottom of the stairs.

In front of him it felt as if a big room opened up. He could only sense that, because he couldn't see a thing. It was pitch black, he could not even see his own hand in front of his face.

'Sit down, there's a mat on the floor,' the witch said in a friendly tone.

'Thank you.' He sat down.

Judging by her voice the witch sounded as if she were around fifty years old and sitting two or three metres away from him.

'How can I help you?'

'I don't really need any help,' the Little Buddha replied. 'I am travelling and today I somehow ended up in your cave, I guess partially due to coincidence and partially out of curiosity.'

He still had to get used to the strange situation. It wasn't every day that he talked to a witch in a cave, in complete and utter darkness.

'People say you are very wise.'

'Yes, they do.'

'So, are you?'

'I don't know. I am able to help many people because I have lived a different and quite unusual life. Because of this I probably appear wise to them.'

She fell silent for a moment.

'As you might have heard already, I am blind.'

The Little Buddha nodded, but then he remembered that it was pitch black and that the witch was blind, so he stopped nodding.

'How do you feel right now?' the witch asked him. 'Without being able to see anything?'

'I feel like I am in a dream. It's strange, I feel much more awake than I do in the darkness that I experience when I close my eyes.'

'Yes, that's a good observation. As if you are experiencing a dream fully conscious. With the difference being that the images are still created in the mind, but not the voices or other sounds.'

The Little Buddha tried to imagine what it would be like to always be surrounded by darkness, just like the witch.

'Aren't you sad sometimes that you are not able to see?' he asked her carefully.

'No, not really. At least not any more. You know, I might not be able to see, but I can hear very well.'

She fell silent for another moment.

'I can even hear what hearts are saying. When they talk about their longings and dreams, about their sufferings and their problems. I think most people come because they want me to bring to light what is hidden deep inside their hearts. They come to the darkness because down here it is impossible to close their eyes to the truth.'

'So what do you do when someone comes to you with a problem? Do you use some magic and make the problem disappear?'

'No, I can't do that,' the witch answered with a laugh. 'That wouldn't be good either. After all you don't go through bad times for no reason.'

She paused. It was as if she wanted him to think for a moment about what she had just said. Then she returned to the Little Buddha's question.

'First of all, I try to make the person understand that they have to accept their problems. This is the most important thing, because only when you accept a problem will you be able to let go of it. I try to encourage everybody to stop ignoring or fighting their problems. If you ignore a problem, it becomes bigger because it starts to scream for attention. If you fight it, it will fight back. So you have to accept it if you ever want to get rid of it. It may seem hard at first, but it's the only way to set it free. Once the problem is free to move about, space is created for a new experience. My mother, who was also a witch, was always happy when somebody came to her with a major crisis. She regarded it as great news. "Something bad is always followed by something good," she used to say.'

The Little Buddha listened carefully, and the witch continued.

'You know, every situation always has two sides to it, a good one and a bad one. Imagine a coin: on one side there's a problem, and on the other side there's a possibility. How you perceive a situation depends on which side you choose to look at. The coin always remains the same.'

He thought of the writing on the stone at the entrance to her cave.

'In life you only ever see what you want to see.'

'I will tell you a story,' the blind witch said. 'A story about the two sides of life. About how you can choose which side you want to experience.'

The Little Buddha beamed with joy in the midst of the darkness.

He loved stories.

*

Once upon a time there was an old man who was teaching his grandchildren about life. He said to them:

'Deep inside of me there is a fight, a terrible fight between two wolves. One wolf represents all bad things – fear, envy, anger, arrogance, greed, lies, ignorance, guilt, inferiority and the ego. The other wolf represents all good things – joy, peace, love, hope, sharing, friendship, compassion, generosity, truth and faith.' He continued: 'The same fight exists deep inside of you too, just as it does in every other person in the world.'

The grandchildren thought about his words, and after a little while one of them had a question for the grandfather.

'So which wolf is going to win?'

The old man answered calmly.

'The one you feed.'

*

How true this story was! The Little Buddha smiled. It was a very special moment that he was experiencing and the words still echoed in his head: 'The one you feed.' Life could be so easy. He smiled even more, and although the blind witch couldn't see his smile in the dark cave, she could feel it. And maybe she could even hear it.

The witch and the Little Buddha talked for a long time. He told her about the experiences he had had so far on his journey, and she told him about her life in the cave. She also spoke about how she had become ill many years ago and how that illness had led to her blindness.

First she had been in a state of shock and despair, but after a while she had learned to accept her fate. She had no other option. But instead of simply trying to survive without her eyesight, she had started to look for the positive side. She hadn't been happy with mere survival, she wanted to be able to really enjoy life. In this way she slowly accessed a wonderful world. A world most people never really experience.

She had been forced to see through the inner eye.

Now the witch used this experience to help those who came to her with seemingly unresolvable problems. She helped them to see what remained hidden from the normal eye: the worries, fears and desires that were slumbering deep down in everybody's soul. She helped to reveal to others that which was hidden by their own blindness.

'That's why I live in this dark cave, so that people are forced to look at life through the inner eye.'

'But can you help everybody?' the Little Buddha wanted to know.

'No, not everybody. Many people expect me to perform miracles on them, to touch them and take all their problems away at once. But life doesn't work like this. You know, everybody is responsible for their own wellbeing. I might be able to tell somebody how to turn a problem into a possibility. I can point out the door, but each person has to open this door and go through it by themselves. It may seem obvious, but wellbeing and happiness require some will, and for some reason there are some people who appear to not really want happiness in their lives.'

They spent the whole evening together in the dark cave, exchanging stories of their lives. Eventually they both grew tired, and so the witch invited the Little Buddha to stay overnight. He gratefully accepted her offer.

'You know,' the witch said just before they both lay down to sleep, 'most people regard me as a wise person because I am an old, blind woman who lives happily in a cave and who says some things that make sense. But they don't understand that words alone don't make somebody wise. After all it's very easy to give out advice; the real challenge is to follow it. True wisdom, therefore, is only born when good advice is put into practice.'

*

When the Little Buddha woke the following morning, he almost fell asleep again straight away. It was still pitch black in the cave, there was no difference between night and day.

'I'd love to stay longer,' he said, 'the quietness feels really good.'

It was true, after his time in the hectic town he was enjoying the stillness of the cave and the woods even more.

'But if I'm honest,' he added, 'it's too dark for me here. I really need some light.'

'I understand that,' the witch said. 'If I still had my eyesight, I wouldn't want to be surrounded by constant darkness either.'

She thought about something else for a moment.

'Maybe you could visit a friend of mine. He doesn't live far from here. If quietness is what you are looking for then you will love his place.'

'Great! How do I find your friend?'

'Go to the old castle that's half a day's walk south of the forest. When you get there simply ask for the gardener. Send him my best regards.'

The Little Buddha thanked her and got up to leave.

'It was really nice that you visited me down here,' the blind witch said.

'Yes, I feel the same.'

He turned around and left this dark, but very special, place.

*

Back at the clearing, the Little Buddha saw that people were already waiting to see the witch. As he passed them with a friendly smile, one of them got up and approached him.

'Have you been healed?'

'Yes,' the Little Buddha replied. 'Although, actually, I hadn't been ill in the first place.'

He started wondering. Some of the people that came to seek help from the witch really seemed to expect that only a few words from the blind woman would be enough to relieve them of all their problems.

Abracadabra, and some magic makes everything good again…

But the Little Buddha knew that this wasn't the case. He had understood what the witch had been trying to tell him:

Good advice will only help you
once you've put it into practice.

Chapter 7
The Patient Gardener

ate in the afternoon, the Little Buddha arrived at the castle. He had imagined it to be huge, with towers and thick walls, but what he actually found looked more like a large country cottage. A nice house without a doubt, but it didn't really look like a castle.

He stepped closer. A few children were playing near the entrance, and a couple of peacocks were proudly tiptoeing on the lawn. The clouds were rolling by slowly, and one could hear the flowing water of a nearby stream. It all seemed very peaceful.

As he didn't see anybody else, the Little Buddha decided to ask the children where he could find the gardener. One of the children, a little girl, showed him a path that led past the house through the garden, and directly to the hut of the gardener. He thanked her for her help and followed the path.

On the way he passed many beautiful trees, bushes and flowers. A wonderful smell filled the air. 'What a lovely place to live,' he thought to himself. 'The people here must be very happy.'

After some time, the Little Buddha reached the hut. He knocked on the door. Nothing. He looked around, but there was no sign of the gardener. He was about to sit down to wait for him when he heard a cheerful whistling in the distance. Feeling curious, he started to walk around the hut and slowly the whistling became louder. Once he got to the other side of the hut, he saw a big vegetable garden in front of him and in the middle of it there was a man, whistling happily, kneeling on the ground, his hands digging in the soil. 'That must be the gardener,' the Little Buddha thought.

When the man noticed the visitor, he got up and came towards the

Little Buddha.

'Hello,' he said with a friendly voice.

'Hello,' the Little Buddha replied. 'I am looking for the gardener.'

The man smiled.

'You are standing right in front of him. How can I help you?'

The Little Buddha told him that he had been with the blind witch in the forest. He gave the gardener her regards and asked if there was any possibility of staying with him for a few days.

'Of course, you can stay as long as you want.'

As if it was the most normal and natural thing in the world to offer to a complete stranger.

'I have a second bed in my hut, so there's no problem. I just have one question: why did the witch send you to me?'

'After having spent quite some time in the hectic town I needed a quiet place. The cave in the forest was really special, but it was too dark for me. So the witch recommended that I come and visit you.'

The gardener smiled again.

'What an excellent recommendation. Make yourself at home.'

*

The Little Buddha stayed for quite some time with the gardener in the castle grounds. He started to meditate regularly again, enjoying the heavenly quietness and the beauty of nature. It was like being at home once more, under his big old Bodhi tree.

During his stay, he sometimes helped the gardener with his work. He watered the flowers, trimmed some trees and bushes and planted new seeds. But sometimes he also just watched the gardener, because the

Little Buddha loved to observe other people.

The gardener was a fascinating person. Whenever he walked through his garden he stopped again and again to watch the plants growing. At least it seemed like this. Some might have said that the gardener worked very slowly, but this wasn't the case; he simply did his work with an incredible inner calmness. Even the Little Buddha was impressed by his serenity. Nothing seemed to be able to unsettle him. Neither the playing children who often made a lot of noise, nor a strong wind or a thunder storm; not even the two castle dogs, who ran again and again through his beautifully kept flower beds, were able to upset him.

'Where do you get all your patience from?' the Little Buddha wanted to know one evening as they sat comfortably around a small open fire outside the hut.

'I don't really know,' the gardener said. 'It's probably the countryside that helps me to be patient. You know, I've lived here all my life. With very few exceptions I am always surrounded by calmness, and so it's only natural for me to be calm as well.'

'I still don't understand how you do it,' the Little Buddha said after a while. 'When I sit under my tree back home, I never have to carry out any important jobs. I have plenty of time to be friendly, to be patient or to be simply calm. You, however, lead a normal life, you have responsibilities and lots of distractions. Every day you have a lot of work to do, yet you still manage always to be friendly, and to have time for everybody and everything. That really puzzles me.'

The gardener knew what the Little Buddha meant, but for him it wasn't puzzling at all.

'I just take the time,' he said after a brief pause.

'And where do you take the time from if there is none?'

'There is always time. It just depends what you do with it.'

The Little Buddha understood what the gardener was saying. After all he had said almost the same words to Mr Singer, the hectic traveller from the big town who had never travelled anywhere. However, he still wasn't satisfied with the answer he got.

'And what if there is an unexpected problem? For example, what if the well is broken and you are busy, all day long, carrying water from the stream? If this happened, where would you get the time from to do all your other jobs?'

'Well, in that case I would only have time to carry the water, that's true. But it wouldn't matter. The question is always what is important in any given moment. Certain problems you simply can't avoid, and so you can only allow them to happen as they do.'

The gardener briefly reflected on his own words.

'Fortunately, the well is not broken every day...'

*

They talked a long time that evening; about the fascinating mystery of time, about problems and possibilities, about calmness and about life.

The following morning, they both strolled in silence through the huge garden of the castle. It had rained during the night, and so the air was even fresher and clearer than usual. It was a beautiful way to wake up.

While they were walking, the gardener started to think about their conversation from the previous evening.

'I think I have learned a lot from nature,' he said.

The Little Buddha wasn't fully awake yet.

'What do you mean?'

'Yesterday you asked me where I get my patience from, didn't you?'

'Yes. And so, where do you get it from?'

'From nature. You see, having patience really means being able to wait; and the ability to wait I have learned from nature.'

The gardener looked around and pointed to a big tree.

'You can spend weeks sitting in front of this tree trying to watch how it grows. At first it would be absolutely in vain, and why? Because the tree grows really, really slowly. So slow in fact that even from one month to the next you wouldn't notice any difference. But the tree is growing all the time, every day a little bit. A big and strong tree like this one simply takes a lot of time to grow. If you plant the seed of such a tree, and you want to see how a tiny seed is transformed into this majestic tree, well then you need a lot of patience. You have to be able to wait.'

The Little Buddha listened carefully and observed the big tree in front of them.

'It's a very similar story with humans,' the gardener continued, 'they too need a lot of time to grow. You know, every person grows with experience, and it takes time to gain this experience. Therefore, we should be patient with people too. We should always be willing to wait until the full potential of each and every one of us unfolds; until we all become our own majestic trees.'

They kept silent again and admired the huge tree.

'It's really a shame that not everybody has as much patience as you do,' the Little Buddha said eventually.

'Patience to allow the good things in life to simply happen.'

*

The Little Buddha stayed many weeks with the gardener. He had a wonderful time throughout, but eventually the day arrived when he wanted to continue his journey.

'Thank you for your hospitality,' he said with a big smile. 'I hope I will return one day to this beautiful place.'

'You are always welcome,' the gardener said, before pausing for a moment. 'I have an idea. Why don't you make a little detour and stop in the village nearby? Go to the bakery at the market square and ask for the baker. If she is not inside baking bread then she is probably sitting outside on her bench, reading a book. Ask her for the secret of her happiness. She will tell you a story.'

The Patient Gardener

Chapter 8
The Happy Baker

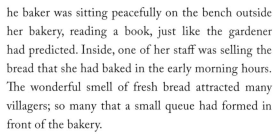

he baker was sitting peacefully on the bench outside her bakery, reading a book, just like the gardener had predicted. Inside, one of her staff was selling the bread that she had baked in the early morning hours. The wonderful smell of fresh bread attracted many villagers; so many that a small queue had formed in front of the bakery.

The Little Buddha watched the baker for a while from the other side of the market square. She spent almost the whole time sitting comfortably on her bench. Either she was reading her book, or she was talking to one of her many friends who came by regularly. Unlike the way it was in the big town, the people in the village all knew each other well.

Whenever the queue in front of the bakery became too long, the baker got up and helped at the counter. She seemed happy and fully satisfied, as if she were consciously enjoying every single moment.

The Little Buddha waited quietly for a while before walking over to her.

'May I sit down?' he asked, pointing to the free space next to her. 'I have a question for you.'

The baker looked up from her book and gave him an inviting smile.

'Of course, take a seat.'

She looked him over from head to toe.

'You seem like somebody who wants to ask me for the secret recipe of my happiness.'

He looked back at her in astonishment.

'How do you know that?' He was puzzled. Maybe the gardener had told her that he was coming. But no, there hadn't been enough time for that.

'Well, you've been standing for more than an hour on the other side of the market, staring at me.'

The Little Buddha blushed.

'Don't worry, it's not a sin to be curious. And besides, everybody else who has come to me to learn about the secret has done the same.'

She drank some mint tea from her beautiful teacup and took a deep breath.

'You know, it's not really a secret. It's just a story, a story about the temptation of postponing your happiness. Do you want to hear it?'

'I'd love to,' the Little Buddha said with excitement.

So the baker put her book to one side and began to tell a true story from her life.

*

Some years ago there was a businessman who had just moved to our village. When he came to my bakery for the first time, he fell in love with my bread straightaway. He adored the fantastic smell and the special taste.

One day I was sitting happily on my bench, just like today, talking to friends and reading a book, when the businessman arrived at the bakery to buy some bread. When he came out again, he sat down next to me.

'You are the baker woman, aren't you?' he asked, and I nodded.

'I have been thinking about your wonderful bread and I had an idea that I would like to put to you.'

'Oh, I always love to hear new ideas,' I said. 'Go ahead.'

The businessman went ahead.

'I have lived in many different towns and villages, and your bread is by far the best bread I have ever tasted.'

I smiled. Compliments like this always felt really good.

The businessman continued.

'Why don't you open another bakery in the next village? Your bread would sell really well in any place. You could teach somebody your art of breadmaking, and then they could bake the bread for you in the other village. If you then employed another person to sell the bread, you would have a second bakery.'

'And then?' I wondered.

'Once the second bakery is also running successfully, you would have to teach various people your art of breadmaking. When you have done that, you could go to a bank, get a loan and open many more bakeries in different towns and villages.'

'And then?'

'One day, when everything is running smoothly, you will earn enough money to employ other people to do all the work. To get to that point you will of course need quite a lot of patience and endurance, it might take a few years or even a decade, but you will see that it's worth it. You will earn a lot of money without having to work for it.'

'And then?'

'Well, then you will have enough time to do all of the things that you really want to be doing.'

'Like what?' I wanted an example.

The businessman thought about it for a moment, and soon he had an idea.

'You could sit here peacefully on your bench and read a good book...'

*

The baker and the Little Buddha both had to smile.
How easy it was to make life complicated.
And how difficult it could be to simply be happy.

Chapter 9
The Doubting Warrior

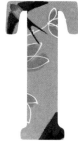he Little Buddha had enjoyed the baker's story. After talking to her further and tasting some of her delicious bread, he set off in the early afternoon to continue his journey. The courageous widow, whom he had met at the beginning of his trip, had told him how beautiful the sea was. As he had never been to the sea, he really wanted to find out for himself.

On foot the journey would have taken him two or even three days, but on the morning of the second day the Little Buddha got lucky and was picked up by a horse-drawn carriage that went all the way to the coast. By noon he would reach his destination.

The big blue sea was awaiting him.

*

The Little Buddha was sitting in the back of the carriage on a bale of straw, watching endless fields of lush green pastures passing by. It felt great to be under way again. 'Travelling is also a form of meditation,' he thought to himself. 'While living fully in the present and enjoying every single moment, time slowly dissolves.'

Next to him sat a middle-aged man. He wore an old robe and had a sword lying by his side. The man was deeply lost in thought.

For a while they sat in silence next to each other, but soon the Little Buddha became curious again.

'Why do you carry a sword?'

The man looked first at his sword, and then at the Little Buddha.

'I'm a soldier. The sword is my weapon.'

'You don't really look like a soldier,' the Little Buddha said, wondering.

'Where are you going to?'

'I am going back to my home town. The war is over, my job is done.'

After many years of fighting, peace finally ruled at the frontiers, and so the warrior was able to return home. Yet instead of seeing signs of relief and joy, the Little Buddha saw deep, sorrowful furrows on the soldier's face.

'You don't seem very happy. Aren't you glad that the war is over?'

'Yes, of course I am.'

For a moment he got lost in thought again.

'The war was absolutely dreadful. I think if you haven't experienced it for yourself, you wouldn't be able to imagine just how terrible it really is.'

He paused.

'People like me who have seen such a tremendous amount of suffering are left with only two possibilities: to either continue fighting because of all the anger and despair that have accumulated, and thus look for new conflicts until the end of our lives, or to never touch a weapon again.

'I have decided to never touch a weapon again. Once I've returned to my home town, I will take my sword and I will drop it as deep into the ocean as I possibly can. I want to have peace in my life, and so yes, I am very happy that the war is over.'

He smiled a little, but his sorrowful furrows remained.

'But you are right,' he continued, 'there is something that clouds my joy. I am really happy that I have survived the war, and that I can return home now, but at the same time I am also worried about the future.'

The Little Buddha gave him a questioning look.

'I just don't know what to do right now. You see, I don't know anything other than how to fight in battles. As a warrior I have always felt very strong, I have always known exactly what had to be done. But now? I don't think I know how to lead a normal life.'

'But you can learn how to do something else now,' the Little Buddha said. 'It's never too late to start something new, to begin again.'

The warrior stared with disbelief into the empty sky.

'But I know only war.'

He seemed weak and insecure.

'I am afraid of the change that lies ahead of me. War is terrible, without a doubt. Every day is dangerous and there is a lot of cruelty, pain and death, but I had gotten used to the danger and even to the horror. It had become something familiar. It might sound strange to you, but the moment when the horror became familiar, I almost stopped being afraid of it.'

For a moment they both listened to the calls of a small flock of birds that was passing close to the carriage.

'I understand that,' the Little Buddha said. 'The unknown always causes more fear than the known; and because of this, change is never an easy thing.'

He thought about the words of the blind witch: *'How you perceive a situation depends on which side of the coin you choose to look at.'* Maybe the warrior simply had to change his perception; to turn the coin around and look at its other side.

'Instead of regarding your situation as a problem that worries you, why don't you look at it as a possibility that gives you hope?'

The warrior thought for a while.

'I know what you mean,' he replied eventually, 'but right now, I find it very difficult to regard my situation as anything other than a problem. After all, who wants to give work to an old soldier?'

His desperation remained unchanged.

The Little Buddha realized that it wasn't always so easy to turn the coin from the negative to the positive side. At least, it wasn't as easy as it had seemed when the witch had talked about it.

*

While they were sitting silently in the back of the rattling carriage, the Little Buddha thought about how he might be able to help his companion. There had to be a way to give him some confidence. Maybe the warrior would be able to find a solution to his problem if he did what he could do best, and that was to see the world through the eyes of a warrior.

'How did you deal with fear before a battle?' he asked him.

'That's a good question.'

The warrior had to think about this for a while. Nobody had ever asked him a question like this.

'There were two things that helped me to overcome my fear before a battle. First of all, it was very important that I didn't look back, not even for a single moment. Once I started to think about all the people who had died the previous day or the previous week, I became paralysed by fear. So my full concentration was focused on the battle that lay ahead of me, I stopped thinking and let myself fall.'

'And what else helped you?'

'Faith in winning. To firmly believe that I would win the battle and return home alive. The stronger this faith was, the less fear I had.'

'But where did you get the conviction from that you would survive the war?' the Little Buddha asked. 'The odds of dying were really high, weren't they?'

'That's right,' the warrior said, 'but if I had thought right from the start that I would die anyway, then it would have been better for me to stay at home. How could I win if I believed from the start that I would lose?'

The Little Buddha understood that it was important to have a positive attitude, but what he didn't understand was how the warrior was able to control what he believed in.

'How was it that you only believed in winning? As a soldier, have you never doubted victory?'

'No, I couldn't allow myself to have any doubts. I needed total clarity and conviction.'

The warrior paused for a moment and thought about his own words. Then he continued:

'In order to strengthen my faith in victory, I always used to imagine exactly what the winning moment would feel like. In my mind I visualized over and over again that I had already won. I literally felt the relief, the glory and the pride. I felt how I cheerfully threw my arms up in the air, again and again, and all the time I tried to make these feelings seem as real and intense as possible.'

He fell silent again for a few moments.

'You know, when it comes to faith and belief, the feeling is the most important thing, because what I feel, I also believe.'

The Little Buddha listened carefully. It all made perfect sense, apart from one thing.

'I wonder why you don't use your warrior qualities to overcome your fear of the changes that lie ahead of you?'

The warrior looked at him in surprise.

'Think about what it is exactly that you want. Set a clear goal. Then, imagine the happy moment when you start working in your desired job for the first time, the moment when you reach your goal. Visualize this successful moment the same way you did before a battle.'

For the first time that day the warrior smiled properly. The Little Buddha was right. The terrible despair that the warrior had felt at the beginning of their conversation had disappeared. Slowly but surely hopefulness was returning.

Because hope felt good, the warrior could also started to believe in his potential again. The more that he believed in his strength, and in his opportunities, the less he feared the changes that were lying ahead of him.

The carriage rolled slowly towards the coast. The air around them became clearer and changed into a pleasant, fresh breeze as they approached the sea. While the warrior was thinking about what kind of job-related goal he should set himself, the Little Buddha meditated; or rather he tried to meditate, because he couldn't quieten his mind. All the time, he too was thinking about the warrior's situation. At some point, a question entered his mind, which he immediately asked the warrior.

'Which job would you choose if you knew that you couldn't fail?'

The warrior stared for a moment at the Little Buddha before he answered.

'Gardener. I think I would like to work as a gardener.'

He was silent for a while; when he continued, he sounded determined.

'For the last two decades I have fought in terrible battles, and I have caused much destruction. I would like to make up for that, at least a little bit. I would like to create something that grows. I want to be surrounded by life, not by death.'

The Little Buddha remembered the patient gardener at the castle.

'I have a friend who is a gardener, maybe you should visit him.' He started daydreaming. 'I think that it's a very nice job. All day long you are outside, in the fresh air, you live with the rhythm of nature, surrounded by happy creatures... I could actually imagine being a gardener myself.'

The warrior smiled contentedly.

'And think about it,' the Little Buddha continued. 'You have survived a long war even though the chances of doing so were very small. So really, why should you fail as a gardener?'

*

They reached the coast in the early afternoon. The horse-drawn carriage stopped and the Little Buddha got off. The warrior had to stay and continue for another half a day to get to his home town, so their paths went in different directions.

Even though it was a very hot day, the warrior didn't mind the long journey that lay ahead of him. He was happy that he had found a goal that he believed in, a goal worth fighting for. And the Little Buddha?

The Little Buddha was absolutely overwhelmed by the sight of the sea. In all his excitement, he almost forgot to say goodbye.

'All the best to you,' he called after the warrior, before running down a big sand dune. He couldn't wait to meet the deep blue sea.

Chapter 10
The Old Fishermen

or the Little Buddha, the encounter with the sea was love at first sight. It was even more impressive than he had imagined it to be. It was big, mysterious and incredibly beautiful. It seemed simple, yet also very powerful. He couldn't believe that he had never been there before. It seemed to him as if he had found a unique treasure; a magical, wonderful treasure that turned every place that was close by into something very special.

Time seemed to stand still. At night, he slept peacefully between two small sand dunes, and the days he spent meditating for hours under a lonely palm tree on the beach. Sometimes, he also went straight into the water to experience the sea even more intensely, to absorb it through all of his senses.

He felt the soft wetness on his skin, he tasted the salt on his lips, and when he breathed deeply, he could smell the fresh coastal air in his nose. He listened to the sounds of the breaking waves, and with his eyes he admired the incredible vastness of this massive, blue desert. Every moment by the sea seemed perfect to him.

*

Soon after his arrival the Little Buddha had noticed a group of five old fishermen who met every day, at the same time, close to the place where he was sleeping. Standing on a big rock they were following their passion and their former trade. They were fishing.

*

For about a week the Little Buddha watched the fishermen from a distance. Every evening they met just before sunset on the big rock. They never arrived together, each one came separately. Once everybody was there, they unpacked their fishing rods, attached the bait to their hooks and finally threw the fishing lines with their hooks and the bait as far as possible into the sea. Then they waited patiently until they caught fish, and in the meantime they watched the slowly setting sun.

Every one of them seemed calm and very happy.

'This has got to have something to do with the sea,' the Little Buddha thought to himself.

One evening he walked over to them: he had grown curious again.

'Hello,' he said in a very friendly way. 'I have been watching you for a while, and I wondered why you all look so happy?'

The fishermen looked at him, and after a few moments of silence one of them said what all of them were thinking.

'We look happy because we are happy.'

'And why are you so happy?'

'That's what we want to be,' another fisherman said with a smile.

There it was again, the will. The blind witch had already told him about it. 'If only it was that easy,' the Little Buddha thought to himself. On his journey he had met and seen quite a few older people, but many of them had seemed rather sad. He doubted that all those people really wanted to be sad, and so he wondered what the old fishermen's secret was.

'So, what exactly do you need if you want to grow old happily?'

For a few moments they were still again, and the gently breaking waves were the only sound to be heard.

'Why don't you sit down first of all,' one of the fishermen said eventually, pointing to a free spot on the rock.

The Little Buddha sat down.

*

Without saying a word, the five fishermen welcomed him. Straightaway he felt at ease in their company. The pleasant calmness that was transmitted by the old men reminded the Little Buddha of his home. The big Bodhi tree was old as well, and so perhaps it was age itself that was transmitting this sense of calm.

'Are you happy because you are old?'

All five fishermen smiled.

'That's a good question,' one of them said. 'I am old and I am feeling happy, but is there any connection between age and happiness? I don't know. If so, then there would have to also be a connection between youth and sadness.' The fisherman paused for a second. 'Do you think that every time you are sad it's because you are young?'

The Little Buddha looked at him in surprise, but quickly he shook his head. 'No,' he thought to himself, 'I have never been sad because I am young.'

Another fisherman continued the conversation.

'I don't think anybody is happy simply because they are old. After all, there are many old people who are terribly sad. Your emotional state, whether you are happy or sad, doesn't depend on your age. It's more the other way round: your true age depends on how you feel. When you are happy, you radiate something fresh, something young. When you are sad however, you appear rather old. Don't you find that sad people usually look much older than happy ones?'

The Little Buddha nodded in agreement. The fisherman was right. Happy people somehow seemed to be more alive. As if they were still much further away from the sadness of death.

*

The fisherman who was standing right next to the Little Buddha started talking.

'Of course, age brings some nice things with it as well. Serenity for example. As a young man I was always worried about many things. About my work, my family, my house, about the weather, about tomorrow and even about God. Instead of worrying about all these things and being concerned about something that hasn't even happened yet, I now simply take things the way they unfold every day. I let life simply be life, without having any expectations; neither good ones nor bad ones.'

He stared thoughtfully at the darkening horizon.

'You know, looking back over my life I recently realized that my expectations have caused me a lot of restlessness. The less I waited for something, the more calmness I found.'

The fisherman looked away from the yellowy-red horizon, and turned to the Little Buddha.

'Deep serenity has to do with age, of that I am sure. I experienced it for the first time when it became clear to me that I don't have any more time to be constantly waiting for the "now" to arrive.'

*

They were all silent for a while. With the calm sea next to them, and the solid rock below, it almost seemed as if they were all meditating together. Then, all of a sudden, the fishing rod of the fisherman who was standing closest to the water, started to move.

'You asked what you need in order to grow old happily?'

He took one step backwards and got a firm hold on his fishing rod.

'It's very simple: a lot of fresh air and even more fresh, delicious food!'

The moment he spoke the last word, he pulled his fishing line quickly out of the water and proudly presented a big, floundering fish.

They all laughed.

'No, wait, I have to correct myself,' the successful fisherman added. 'Not only do you need fresh air and delicious food, but every day you also have to laugh out loud at least once!'

He was right, the Little Buddha thought.

Although it was so easy and so important, most people, the world over, didn't laugh enough.

*

One of the other fishermen continued the conversation.

'I think in order to stay happy when growing old, you have to keep moving: your body, your mind and also your heart, like a river that never stops flowing. Take us as an example: we can't spend the whole day out on the sea any more like we used to. We are not strong enough now for that. Fortunately, our children and grandchildren look after us, so we don't have to work. But that doesn't mean that we want to stop fishing. After all, we have fallen in love with our work over the years, why should we give it up now? So, instead, we meet here every evening. The daily walk to the sea keeps our bodies alive, the conversations keep our minds active and being with friends moves our hearts.'

'That's true,' the fisherman, who stood right next to the Little Buddha said, 'but there is something else: the most important thing is that you keep your curiosity, and that you never stop learning. As long as you stay curious, you will keep on discovering things in life that make you happy. You travel, for example, and so every day you experience something new. Every day, you learn something about life. We too learn something new every day, because the sea is a teacher with endless knowledge. If you are patient and attentive, it will share all its wisdom with you.'

A huge wave came rolling towards them and crashed on the rock.

'You know,' the oldest of the fishermen said, 'there are a thousand good reasons to be happy, no matter whether you are old or young. But for me, one thing is clearly the most important.' He paused for a moment. 'And that's the people who I love: my family, my friends, even the strangers who I don't know yet who might become my friends one day. I am grateful that I have met all of these people in my life, because every single one of them gives me a new reason to be happy every day.'

*

They watched in silence as the last rays of sunlight disappeared behind the horizon. It was a wonderful evening; the kind you wished would never end.

The Little Buddha thought about the fishermen and about growing old. The situation of an old person could actually be compared to a sunset. It was beautiful, maybe even the most beautiful part of the day; the most beautiful part of life. Free from expectations and filled only with calmness. A moment that brought to mind all good things and that made you forget all bad things.

The sunset, however, also evoked a feeling of melancholy; a feeling that something was going to end. Fearing the end, many old people tried to prolong the sunset of life as much as possible. Almost in a state of panic they climbed up a mountain to be able to see the sun just a little longer. Instead of sitting down and enjoying the special moment, they desperately tried to stop the time that remained, and while they did so the special moment passed them by almost unnoticed.

The old fishermen, on the other hand, seemed to accept that growing old and death were a part of life, and because they accepted it, they were able to enjoy their remaining time much more. Maybe that's why they were so happy.

As the rock sank into the darkness and it slowly got colder, the fishermen packed up their gear and started to go home. The Little Buddha thanked them for the pleasant and inspiring evening and said goodbye. Just before he went, the oldest of the fishermen turned around to him.

'There is something we haven't talked about yet.'

The Little Buddha looked at him in suspense.

'If you want to grow old happily,' the old man said with a calm voice, 'you must never ever stop dreaming.'

A hint of magic was in the air.

'Because when you stop dreaming, it's time to die.'

Chapter 11
The Rich Peasant Woman

**T**he Little Buddha spent many more evenings with the old fishermen on the rock, and many more times he watched the yellow sun turn red and slowly sink into the sea. He loved the beach so much that he could almost have stayed there forever.

But at some point, he started to miss his big old Bodhi tree. Although he was still happy by the coast, he found himself thinking more and more often about his home. More and more often, he let his hand slip into his shoulder bag to touch the white stone he had brought. His holiday had already lasted over two months and maybe that was enough.

He decided to slowly end his journey and to head home.

*

Saying farewell to the sea was very difficult for the Little Buddha – leaving special places and good friends behind was never easy. His only consolation was the thought of coming back soon.

The morning of his departure arrived, and he said goodbye to the fishermen who had come to wish him all the best for his remaining trip. Then he took a final look at the sea and set off.

Instead of returning along the same route, though – passing the endless fields, through the dark forest and through the big town – the Little Buddha started heading exactly in the opposite direction. There was another way to get to his Bodhi tree that was much quicker. The only problem was that this way took three days travelling through a big desert, so a long and lonesome walk was ahead of him. A walk from the blue to the yellow desert.

Having spent a lot of time with many different people during the last weeks and months, he actually didn't mind the solitude at all. On the contrary, he enjoyed being able to quietly reflect on all of his experiences. Soon, however, he had to realize that he was about to face a completely different problem. The Little Buddha had totally underestimated the extreme heat of the vast desert.

Even before the sun had reached its highest point, he was hardly able to put his feet on the burning sand. It seemed to him as if everything around him was on fire, it was so hot. He could hardly stop drinking and soon, in an attempt to satisfy his ever-increasing thirst, shortly after noon, all his water had gone. He was feeling hotter all the time and, as the walking became harder and harder, he also slowed down more and more. Desperately he looked around to see whether he could find some shade somewhere, but without success. Here and there he saw a small stone or a dried-out bush, but otherwise there was only yellow, burning sand.

It was the first time during his journey that the Little Buddha felt fear. He didn't know what to do, how to escape from this situation. In his search for shade, he had turned around on his own axis so many times that he didn't know in which direction he was supposed to walk any more. He had totally lost his orientation. Naturally he tried to stay calm by doing some walking meditation, but it didn't help. His thirst, the overwhelming heat and his fear remained.

Suddenly everything went black and he lost consciousness.

*

When he woke again, the Little Buddha heard children playing and birds singing. A light, cooling breeze touched his burning skin. He opened his eyes and saw that he was lying under a roof of palm leaves.

Slowly he sat up.

'Here, drink something.' A woman passed him a wooden jug filled with fresh coconut milk.

'Thank you,' the Little Buddha said. He was terribly thirsty and drank the whole jug all at once. Then he looked around.

He saw a seemingly endless number of palm trees and lots of mud huts scattered in between. In every corner, there were big clay jugs filled with water. People in colourful clothes were walking about and he was able to make out a massive sand dune in the far distance behind the palm trees.

'Where am I?' he asked, confused.

'In an oasis,' the woman replied in a beautifully soft voice.

The Little Buddha tried to remember what had happened but, as much as he tried, his memory stayed empty. Why was he there?

'You lost consciousness and collapsed in the middle of the desert,' the woman said finally. 'If I hadn't passed you by chance with my goats, you would have died either of thirst, or from the heat of the sun, or both.'

He stared at her, not knowing what to say.

'You were extremely lucky,' the woman continued, 'normally the desert doesn't forgive any mistakes.'

Silence ruled for a moment. The children had stopped playing. Only the light wind and a few birds were to be heard.

'What did I do wrong?' he asked her.

The woman was surprised by this question.

'You were all alone, without shoes and with only one bottle of water, in the middle of the desert. So, unless you were planning to kill yourself, you did pretty much everything wrong that could have been done wrong.'

The Little Buddha didn't know what to say. Of course he hadn't wanted to kill himself.

'I just wanted to take a shortcut home. I didn't expect it to be so hot.'

Slowly but surely he realized that he had been very naive and careless.

The woman shook her head while giving him a motherly smile. The Little Buddha was not the first one to have underestimated the desert. Many people thought they could easily pass through it. After all, the desert appeared to be quite innocent and harmless.

Suddenly her soft and friendly voice changed to a serious tone.

'A shortcut requires your full attention, too. Just because one way is shorter than another, doesn't mean that it will get you to your destination more easily. Let this be a lesson to you. Every path in life deserves the same respect and attentiveness.'

*

The Little Buddha's original plan had fallen to pieces. Instead of getting back home to his Bodhi tree as quickly as possible he was forced to stay a few days at the oasis. He was still too weak to continue the strenuous trip through the desert. Furthermore, the woman had told him that he shouldn't continue his journey all by himself. Within a few days a caravan of merchants would pass through the oasis, and it would be much safer for him to cross the remaining part of the desert in their company. He didn't really have any other choice than to wait patiently for the caravan.

*

During the mornings, the Little Buddha relaxed under one of the many palm trees, to recover and to gain the strength needed for the remaining part of the trip. In the afternoons, he spent most of the time with the woman who had rescued him. She was a peasant, a simple farmer, just like most other residents of the oasis. Together with her husband and their two children she owned a piece of land where they grew fruit and vegetables, and they also had a small herd of ten goats, which gave them fresh milk. Every afternoon, the peasant woman took her goats into the desert, and the Little Buddha accompanied her while waiting for the caravan. Apart from being in good company, it was also a good opportunity for him to get used to the desert climate.

One day, they climbed the big sand dune on their way back. After reaching the top, they stayed for a while to enjoy the fantastic view. From a distance, the oasis appeared to be even more peaceful than it was when you were in it. Almost like a small, green island, it was embedded in a sea of sand. Like a little paradise in the middle of nowhere. Apart from the oasis, there was indeed nothing else. Just sand, as far as the eye could see.

'The desert really has a lot in common with the sea,' the Little Buddha thought to himself. The simplicity, the vastness, the beauty and the stillness, and also the slumbering power, all these things made both the sea and the desert something very special.

Yet, at the same time, they were both able to cause rather unpleasant feelings too. The wild storms that terrified even the hardest and strongest of men. The endless monotony that could drive any person to the most violent insanity, and of course the silent emptiness that could make you feel as if you were the only person on Earth.

'Have you never felt lonely here?' the Little Buddha asked the woman.

'No, I have my family and most of my friends here, so loneliness is

not a problem. When I was younger, however, I was terribly bored. Back then, it seemed to me that every day was the same. Always the same activities, always the same faces. I was constantly surrounded by sun, sand and palm trees, it drove me crazy.'

The peasant woman paused for a moment and glanced across the horizon.

'I hated it so much that at one point I couldn't bear it any more.'

'What did you do?' the Little Buddha asked curiously.

'I went to the town to experience a different life.'

*

While they were standing on the top of the huge sand dune, staring at the horizon and half daydreaming, the woman told the Little Buddha about some of her experiences in the town.

'I spent two exciting years there. Two years that I wouldn't want to change for anything. I met lots of new people and every day I saw and experienced many new things. After some time, I found a good job and I earned enough money to rent a nice house and to do all of the things that I had always wanted to do. I was leading exactly the life that I had dreamt of when I had been in the desert.

'Eventually I started to get bored in the town as well though. I still had enough money to live a nice life, but I wasn't happy. The early days and nights of excitement became unattractive repetitions. For a while I considered moving to a different town, but I had the feeling that this wouldn't make me any happier either. So, in the end I returned to the desert. I went back to my family, to my old friends, the sun, the sand and the palm trees. I returned home.'

She paused. Only the wind of the desert was to be heard in the silence.

'Looking back, I am glad that I went to the town. As I said, I had some good times, but the most important thing was that the experience showed me what a special life I had back here at the oasis. Strange as it is, I think sometimes you have to go away to start loving what you have left behind.'

*

The Little Buddha thought about his own home. Only a few months ago he had been so frustrated because of his constant solitude, that he had no longer seen all of the nice things his home had to offer. Now, however, he was really looking forward to returning. It seemed that sometimes it was indeed the best thing to go away for a while; to have a little break so that you can again appreciate all of the things you have started to take for granted.

*

'You know,' the woman continued, 'out here in the desert I lead a very simple life. Many people from the town would even consider me to be a very poor person. I have hardly any money, and only very few possessions.'

She began to smile contentedly.

'But to me it doesn't matter at all. Because when it comes to experiencing proper wealth, money is of no use anyway. Sure, it makes certain things easier, but it doesn't help anybody to become rich.'

'So what is it that makes somebody rich?' the Little Buddha asked.

'Love,' the peasant woman said. 'Love makes everybody rich, and as you can't buy love it doesn't matter how much money you have.'

Her eyes followed an eagle that was gliding peacefully through the sky.

'Do you know when you are really rich?'

She stopped watching the eagle and turned again to the Little Buddha.

'When you have enough love to be able to give some of it to others. When you are grateful, when you share, trust and respect. When you show love to your fellow human beings, to nature and to all life.'

Silence ruled again. The setting sun was slowly touching the horizon.

'And you? Do you feel rich?'

'Yes,' the woman answered without hesitating.

'I love and I am loved. That means I am rich. Of course, I could strive to have more money and more possessions, but that wouldn't make me any richer.'

The Rich Peasant Woman
111

Chapter 12
A Mighty King

he caravan arrived one week later. Once the merchants, the camel drivers and the camels had rested for a day, the last leg of the Little Buddha's journey began. He thanked the rich peasant woman for the time that they had spent together, and of course also for saving his life. Then he climbed on one of the camels and disappeared with the caravan into the desert.

*

The sun burned fiercely again, almost as if it wanted to melt the earth, but fortunately this time the Little Buddha was better prepared. The peasant woman had given him a turban and a long robe to protect him from the direct sunlight, and also plenty of water. Another big difference was that this time, he didn't have to walk strenuously through the deep sand. Instead he sat high up on a camel, a comfortable distance away from the scorching ground.

He was riding between one of the four camel drivers on one side, and a well-fed merchant on the other. Unfortunately, the merchant was in a bad mood. While the Little Buddha and the camel driver were having a stimulating conversation, the merchant didn't say one word. He didn't even seem to be listening. Once in a while he grumbled something, but nobody understood him.

'Do you know why he is in such a bad mood?' the Little Buddha asked the camel driver in a whisper.

'Because we are running late, by more than a week. We should have already crossed the desert a long time ago.'

The camel driver shrugged his shoulders.

'I personally think that it doesn't really matter, but many of the merchants are very impatient people. If something takes longer than originally planned, they get into a very bad mood very quickly.'

'So why is the caravan running late?' the Little Buddha enquired.

'Some of the camels were ill which meant that we couldn't set off in time. You know, I understand that this is quite annoying for the merchants. They have to get their goods to the market towns as quickly as possible to be able to sell them. But I think they could be more relaxed, at least occasionally. They should have more respect for nature and be a bit more humble. Many of the merchants know a lot of things, but they still have to learn that sometimes it is necessary to simply accept the way things unfold; to take life as it comes. Even if you don't always understand everything, most things in life happen for a good reason.'

'What do you mean?'

'What do I mean? Well, maybe our delay was meant to happen.'

The Little Buddha looked at him, still wondering.

'I will tell you a story,' the camel driver said, 'then you will understand what I mean.'

*

A long, long time ago, a mighty king ruled a huge country. He was a good king. He helped the people as much as he could, and he made sure that there was peace in every corner of his land. The king was respected by everybody. He was a friendly king, yet at the same time, he could also be very strict. Nobody dared say anything bad about him, because nobody wanted to be out of favour with or punished by him.

The king had countless ministers who worked for him. After all, he needed help to manage the huge kingdom. One of his ministers was particularly close to him. Over the years a friendship had developed between them, but unfortunately their friendship had caused some envy amongst the other residents of the royal palace. Quite often the envious ones tried to make the favourite minister less popular with the king, but they were never successful.

One day the king was having his hair cut. He was sitting peacefully in his chair when, all of a sudden, the scissors slipped out of the hand of the royal barber and the king's right ear was cut off. The king was furious. How could that happen?

Quickly the news of the severed royal ear spread throughout the palace. Some of the envious ones also heard about it, and they decided to tell the news to the king's favourite minister. They found him in his house and told him about the ear. The minister listened carefully, then he said: 'Whatever God does is only for the best.'

The envious ones saw their chance. They went straight to the king and told him about the reaction of his favourite minister. 'What?' the king said angrily. 'How dare he say that there is anything good about me losing my ear!' The king was so angry that he ordered his guards to throw the minister in prison. The envious ones could hardly hide their victorious smiles.

And thus it came to pass that the minister was in prison with only bread to eat and water to drink. Many of his friends and colleagues came to visit him. It wasn't a pleasant sight that they were met with. The minister's cell was tiny, dark and dirty, and also the minister himself had started to take on certain qualities of his cell. It was only natural that his friends and colleagues became concerned. Yet every time they asked him how he was, the minister said: 'I am well, and I know that whatever God does is only for the best.'

And indeed, he didn't seem dispirited at all.

The idea that the minister was feeling well upset the envious ones. They went to the king again and told him the words of his favourite minister. 'Well,' the king said, 'if he thinks that it is best for him to be in prison then he may as well stay there.'

This put a smile back on the faces of the envious ones. But though the minister had to stay in prison, his attitude didn't change. Still he continued to say that God's actions are always for the best.

Some weeks passed, and gradually the hunting season arrived. The king was a very passionate hunter too. One morning he set off into the forest but, when the night closed in, the king was attacked by bandits; at least that was what he thought at first. Soon it emerged that the bandits were in fact cannibals. They weren't interested in the king's gold but in his flesh.

They dragged him to their hidden camp where a huge cauldron was already standing on a fire. They prepared the king to be cooked. Just moments before his life was to end, the cannibals' medicine man came to examine him from head to toe. Then, all of a sudden, there were a lot of whispers amongst the cannibals, and within a few moments the king was set free again.

What had happened?

Well, there was a cannibalistic 'law of purity' which said that only those humans whose bodies were absolutely immaculate were allowed to be eaten. When the medicine man had examined the king, he had seen that one ear was missing, and therefore the king had become useless to the cannibals. So the king had just escaped the huge cauldron.

Back in his palace the king remembered the words of his minister. His longstanding friend had been right, if the barber hadn't cut off his ear accidentally he would now be inside the cannibals' stomachs. The king immediately ordered the minister to be freed from prison and to be brought to see him. He told the minister about what had happened in the forest and he *admitted that he had done him wrong. Nevertheless, he still wasn't completely convinced by the words of his favourite minister.*

'I understand now that losing my ear was indeed the best for me, but why was it good for you to spend many weeks in prison?'

'This question I can answer very easily,' the minister said. 'You see, normally I would have joined you on your hunt, and so the cannibals would have captured me as well. You got away with your life because you had an ear missing, but my body is in an immaculate state, and so I would have passed the purity test of the cannibals and would have been cooked.

'As you can see now, whatever God does is only for the best!'

*

The camel driver and the Little Buddha were silent for a few moments while they rode slowly through the desert.

'Do you know now what I mean when I say that our delay might have been meant to happen?'

The Little Buddha nodded.

'If we had set off on time,' the camel driver continued, 'then maybe we would have ended up in a terrible sand storm, or perhaps bandits would have attacked us. Or imagine if the camels had fallen ill on the way and we had been stuck in the middle of the desert.'

'But maybe nothing would have happened,' the Little Buddha commented carefully. 'Who knows.'

He took a big sip of water from his bottle and looked to his right to see if the merchant was listening, but he wasn't. The moody man had fallen asleep on his rocking camel.

'You are right, who knows what would have happened,' the camel driver said. 'But what might have happened or not isn't important anyway. We will never know. The only thing that is important is to trust. To let go and to trust that everything happens for a reason.'

'I know what you are saying, but I think that most people have to first understand something by using their reason before they can trust it, and so I wonder how they are supposed to trust a power that even a mighty king hardly understands...'

'Yes, that's a difficult one, I admit that. But then, this actually illustrates the whole problem: you can't trust using your reason. You can only trust with your heart.'

The camel driver let his sight drift towards the horizon.

'I might not always understand why something happens, but nevertheless it happens. So instead of trying desperately to understand it, I prefer to simply trust. Of course, this is not always easy, because blind trust requires a lot of courage, but my humble experience has shown me that it's worth finding this courage because trust is one of the most powerful and most beautiful feelings that exists; a feeling that you can't understand, but that you don't have to understand either.

'I therefore close my eyes and trust that everything will only happen for the best.'

A Mighty King
121

Chapter 13
The Sad Clown

fter travelling for three long days through the desert, and another half a day through the hills that stood beyond the desert, the Little Buddha finally arrived home. When he saw the big old Bodhi tree from a distance he began jumping for joy. It felt great to be in a familiar place again after such a long time. He enjoyed every single moment of his return.

*

The days passed, and soon he had been home for a whole week. Once the euphoria of returning had worn off, the Little Buddha started to think a lot about his journey; about all the good times he had experienced, about the special places and the unique people. He wondered what was better: to finally return home after having been away for a few months, or to set off into the unknown after having spent a long time in a familiar place.

He thought about the difference between a lake and a river. Meditating under his Bodhi tree resembled the stillness of a clear lake up in the mountains. Every moment was filled with complete calm, and a state of perfect balance prevailed. Travelling, however, had the dynamics of a river: never in one place for long, always on the move, sometimes fast, sometimes slow, but always flowing on and on. The downside was that this constant change used up a lot of energy, but the endless possibilities also made life very exciting: like a wild river that is not really any better but is generally more attractive than a peaceful lake. At least at first sight.

*

In addition to the wonderful and constant change, however, there was something else that the Little Buddha missed even more: his new friends. It was they who had accompanied him on his way to happiness. From them he had learnt what it means to have good friends, and what really matters in life.

Many of the people whom he had met on his journey had become part of his life. The courageous widow, the unsuccessful merchant, the blind witch and the patient gardener. He even missed the hectic Mr Singer and of course, also the happy baker, the doubting warrior and the group of old fishermen. He thought about the rich peasant woman and the camel driver, and about all the stories he had been told by all of these people. Every single farewell had been so difficult for him.

Another week passed, and although the Little Buddha was happy to be back home under his Bodhi tree, he continued to think back wistfully about his journey and his friends. Then, one morning, he was visited unexpectedly by the postman, who had a letter for him. It was the first time that he had ever received something by post.

He opened it in excitement, wondering who could have sent him this letter. He took out a beautiful sheet of paper and began to read what was written on it:

'Dear friend, I hope you are well. Since you left, I have written quite a lot, my book is already half finished. In between I even had some time to write a few poems, and one of these poems was inspired by you and your travels. You'll find it at the end of this letter. I hope you like it.

May our paths meet again very soon.'

The letter was from the merchant in the town. It was exactly what the Little Buddha needed: a few words from a good friend.

He continued to read, curious to find out about the poem.

A clown once lived a travelling life
And walked his path alone,
But deep inside his heart he kept
The part of him called home.

Free as a river, light as air,
From place to place he'd drift,
To clown for people everywhere
With laughter as his gift.

But all his gifts of happiness
Did not return in kind,
As every time he travelled on
He left his friends behind.

When crossroads pointed different ways,
And old paths turned to new,
The part inside his heart called home
Was always torn in two.

Until one golden autumn day,
He heard an old man's song:
'True friendships last a lifetime,
So, be sad, but not for long!'

'Like spokes within a rolling wheel,
Those friends will all remain,
To keep you on your road until
Their turn comes round again.'

The Little Buddha smiled. 'How comforting those words are,' he thought to himself.

For a moment he was happy again, and nothing else mattered under his big old Bodhi tree other than each moment.

These friends will all remain. Knowing this – or, even better, feeling this – was really good.

'Well,' he continued thinking.

'Until the next time.'

The End

How was the book?
Please post your feedback:
#LittleBuddha

AMMONITE
PRESS

www.ammonitepress.com